Charlie and the Chocolate Factory

LEVEL 5

Re-told by: Melanie Williams
Series Editor: Melanie Williams

Pearson Education Limited
Edinburgh Gate, Harlow,
Essex CM20 2JE, England
and Associated Companies throughout the world.

ISBN: 978-1-4479-3136-2

This edition first published by Pearson Education Ltd 2014

1 3 5 7 9 10 8 6 4 2

Set in 15/19pt OT Fiendstar
Printed in China
SWTC/01

Published by Pearson Education Ltd in association with
Penguin Books Ltd, a Penguin Random House company.

For a complete list of the titles available in the Penguin Kids series please go to www.penguinreaders.com.
Alternatively, write to your local Pearson Education office or to: Penguin Readers Marketing Department,
Pearson Education, Edinburgh Gate, Harlow, Essex CM20 2JE, England.

CHAPTER 1

This is a story about a small boy whose name is Charlie Bucket. Charlie lived with his family in a little wooden house near a big town. The house only had two rooms and only one bed, so it was very, very small!

There were six people in his family. Two of them were Mr and Mrs Bucket, Charlie's mother and father.

The other four people who lived in the house were Charlie's grandparents. Because they were all so old and so tired, they stayed in bed all day.

Grandpa Joe and Grandma Josephine slept on one side of the bed.

Grandpa George and Grandma Georgina slept on the other side of the bed.

Mr and Mrs Bucket and Charlie slept in the other room on the floor. In winter it was very cold.

CHAPTER 2

Charlie's family was very poor. Mr Bucket worked in a factory and he did not bring home a lot of money. There was not enough money to buy good food for them all. His mother tried hard to make nice meals. But every day it was cabbage or more cabbage. Charlie was always hungry and he dreamed of eating something else. Most of all, he dreamed of eating *chocolate*!

CHAPTER 3

In Charlie's town, near his house, there was an enormous chocolate factory. It was the biggest and the most famous chocolate factory in the world. It was Mr Willy Wonka's chocolate factory. Every day, when Charlie walked to and from school, he walked past the factory. He always walked very slowly with his nose high in the air. Then he could smell the delicious chocolate smell.

His one wish was to go inside the chocolate factory.

CHAPTER 4

One day, Mr Bucket came home from work. He was very excited.

'Listen, Charlie,' he said. 'Five Golden Tickets. Each one is inside a bar of Wonka chocolate. If you find one, you can visit the factory!'

'But I only get one bar of chocolate a year on my birthday,' said Charlie. 'I'll never find it.'

The next day, a greedy boy called Augustus Gloop found the first ticket.

Here is Augustus with his mother.

CHAPTER 5

The next lucky child was Veruca Salt. Her parents were very rich so they bought thousands of Wonka bars. Mr Salt took the bars to his factory and his workers opened them.

Veruca just lay down on the floor. She kicked her legs and shouted 'Where's my Golden Ticket? I want my Golden Ticket!'

After four days, a worker found a Golden Ticket.

'Give it to me quickly,' Veruca said.

Here is Veruca with her parents.

CHAPTER 6

It was Charlie's birthday. Every year, his family gave him a delicious bar of Wonka chocolate.

'Perhaps I'll be lucky and I'll find a Golden Ticket inside,' Charlie thought.

Charlie held his present carefully in his hands. The four old people sat in the bed and watched.

'Just forget about those Golden Tickets and enjoy the chocolate,' said Grandpa Joe.

Charlie started to open his present.

CHAPTER 7

Charlie did not find a ticket.

Violet Beauregarde found the Third Golden Ticket.

'I usually chew gum,' Violet shouted to the cameras. 'When I read about the Golden Tickets, I started eating chocolate! I found the ticket and now I'm chewing gum again! I *love* gum. At night, I put the gum on the end of my bed. Then in the morning I start chewing it again.'

'What a horrible child,' said Grandma Georgina.

CHAPTER 8

'Listen, it's here in the newspaper,' Mr Bucket said. 'A lucky boy called Mike Teavee found the Fourth Golden Ticket. Mike's crazy about television. He watches it all the time. When people try to talk to him, he shouts, "Go away. Can't you see? I'm watching television!" '

'That's enough', said Grandma Josephine. 'I don't want to hear any more.'

'Another horrible child,' said Grandma Georgina.

'And now there's only *one ticket left,*' said Grandpa George.

CHAPTER 9

Weeks passed. No lucky child found the Fifth Golden Ticket. Where was it?

One afternoon, Charlie was on his way home from school. He was cold and tired and very hungry. Suddenly, he saw something shiny in the street, in the snow. He picked it up. It was some money. It was a silver coin! He could buy *food*.

'I must give it to my mum,' he thought.

'But first, perhaps I'll ...'

CHAPTER 10

Charlie wanted some chocolate – just one bar. He was *so* hungry.

Charlie went into a shop. He gave the man his silver coin and the man gave him a bar of Wonka chocolate.

Charlie quickly pulled off the paper and ate the chocolate. It was *so* delicious.

'One more bar, please,' Charlie said to the man.

Charlie quickly pulled off the paper. This time there was something yellow under the paper ...

CHAPTER 11

Charlie ran all the way home.

'Mother, mother, mother,' shouted Charlie. 'Look! I found some money in the street. I bought two bars of chocolate ... and I found it. It's the Fifth Golden Ticket! It's mine!'

Grandpa Joe sat up in bed, put his arms in the air and shouted 'YIPPEEEEEEEE!' He forgot about his soup!

Then Grandpa Joe jumped onto the floor and started dancing.

CHAPTER 12

Next day was the *big* day. It was a lovely cold, sunny morning. There were hundreds of people outside Wonka's famous factory. It was very early. People pushed and shouted. They wanted to see the five lucky children.

'Stand back! Stand back!' said a police officer when a line of parents and children walked past.

Veruca came first with her rich parents.

Next came Mike with his parents. He looked like an actor in a film!

Behind Mike was the greedy boy, Augustus, with his parents.

Behind Augustus was Violet with her parents.

'Look, she's still chewing gum,' a person in the crowd said.

'I started chewing this piece of gum three months ago!' Violet answered.

Charlie and Grandpa Joe were at the end of the line.

'Who's the thin boy with the old man?' a person in the crowd asked.

'That's Charlie Bucket and his Grandpa Joe,' another person answered.

CHAPTER 13

It was 10 o'clock. It was time to begin. But where was Mr Willy Wonka?

'There he is!' a person in the crowd shouted. 'That's him!'

And so it was!

All eyes turned towards the funny little man with his pointed beard and black hat.

'My *dear* children,' he said. 'How good to see you all. Show me your Golden Tickets. Excellent! And these are your parents? How *nice*! Come in!'

CHAPTER 14

It was nice and warm inside the factory.

'I have to keep it warm for the workers,' Mr Wonka said.

'Who are the workers?' asked Augustus.

'You'll find out soon,' said Mr Wonka.

It was a fantastic place! There were green fields, tall trees, beautiful flowers and a river made of chocolate.

'Look! Near the waterfall!' said Veruca. 'Are they people?'

'Yes, they are,' said Mr Wonka. 'They're the Oompa-Loompas. They're famous for working, dancing and singing.'

The Oompa-Loompas sang and danced and all the children and their parents, and Grandpa Joe, watched.

'Daddy,' shouted Veruca. 'I want an Oompa-Loompa. I want to take it home with me.'

'Not now, my dearest,' her father said.

'Augustus,' shouted Mrs Gloop. 'Don't do that!'

Augustus was on his stomach by the chocolate river. He wanted to taste it!

'Be careful! You'll fall in!' shouted Mr Gloop.

Too late! Augustus was in the river.

CHAPTER 16

'Augustus! Where's Augustus?' cried Mrs Gloop. 'He can't swim.'

'He's going to be fine,' answered Mr Wonka.

'Please take Mr and Mrs Gloop to the Fudge Room,' Mr Wonka said to one of the Oompa-Loompas. 'Their son Augustus is there.'

'Into the boat,' shouted Mr Wonka. 'Off we go. Down the chocolate river.'

Everything in this fantastic world was made of sugar. The pink boat was sugar!

CHAPTER 17

Mr Wonka put a cup into the chocolate river and gave it to Charlie. 'Drink this,' he said. 'You look hungry.'

It was delicious.

'Stop the boat,' Mr Wonka shouted.

'This is the most important room in the factory,' said Mr Wonka. 'Come inside!'

Charlie looked round the enormous room. There were pots everywhere.

'This is the room where we make new sweets. All of you, please do be careful. Don't knock anything over,' said Mr Wonka.

CHAPTER 18

Mr Wonka took them into the middle of the room. There was a great big metal machine. It moved up and down, making a very loud noise.

Suddenly, something small and grey came out. It looked like paper.

'Is that all?' asked Mike.

'Yes, that's all,' answered Mr Wonka. 'Do you know what it is?'

'It's chewing gum!' Violet shouted.

'That's right,' said Mr Wonka. 'The most fantastic gum in the world!'

'This piece of gum is a *meal*,' said Mr Wonka. 'It tastes of soup, meat and blueberry pie.'

'What do you mean, soup, meat and blueberry pie?' asked Violet.

'Well, if you start chewing it, you taste soup, then ...'

'I want it,' said Violet. She put the gum in her mouth and started chewing.

Delicious!

'Help!' cried her mother. 'She's turning purple and ...'

'... round,' said Mr Wonka. 'She's a blueberry! Oompa-Loompas, take her away!'

CHAPTER 20

The next stop was the Nut Room.

'Have a look through the window, but don't go in,' said Mr Wonka. 'The squirrels are opening the nuts.'

'I want a squirrel!' shouted Veruca, looking in the window.

'Don't be silly,' said Mrs Salt. 'These are Mr Wonka's squirrels.'

'But I want one,' Veruca shouted, 'and I'm going to get one *now*.'

She ran into the room. But the squirrels caught *her* and pushed her down a hole.

CHAPTER 21

There were only two children left now – Mike and Charlie.

'Shall we go?' said Mr Wonka.

'Yes,' cried Charlie and Grandpa Joe.

'I'm tired,' said Mike. 'I want to watch television.'

'Let's take the lift if you're tired,' said Mr Wonka. 'This lift can go up and down and round corners. And the walls are glass so you can see out. You can visit any room in the factory.'

The visitors stepped out of the lift into a white room. Mr Wonka gave them all dark glasses.

'That's better,' said Grandpa Joe. 'It was too white.'

'This is where we test our Television Chocolate,' said Mr Wonka.

'What do you mean?' asked Mike.

'Well, I can send a bar of chocolate from one end of the room to the other – by television!' said Mr Wonka.

'That's not possible,' said Mike.

'No? Watch this!' said Mr Wonka.

CHAPTER 23

Six Oompa-Loompas put a *big* bar of chocolate under a camera. They pulled the switch. The chocolate was not there.

'It's in the television!' laughed Charlie. 'It's smaller!'

'I want to be on TV!' shouted Mike.

He ran across the room to the camera and pulled the switch.

'Where's Mike?' shouted Mrs Teavee.

'He's in the television,' answered Mr Wonka.

'He's so small!' cried Mrs Teavee.

'The Oompa-Loompas will make him big again,' said Mr Wonka.

CHAPTER 24

'How many children are there left now?' asked Mr Wonka.

'There's only Charlie left now, Mr Wonka,' said Grandpa Joe.

Mr Wonka turned to look at Charlie and said, 'Are you the only one left?'

'Well, yes,' said Charlie quietly.

'But my *dear boy*,' cried Mr Wonka, 'then you're the *winner*! Well done! Now we must be quick. Jump into the lift, my boy, and you too, Grandpa Joe.'

The lift flew up into the sky.

CHAPTER 25

'We must go down and look at our friends before we go,' said Mr Wonka.

He pushed a different button and the lift flew down.

Now Charlie could see the four children and their parents.

'Are the children going to be all right?' asked Charlie.

'Yes, they'll be fine,' answered Mr Wonka. 'I'm going to give them some sweets to take home. But I have something important to talk to you about, Charlie.'

CHAPTER 26

'I love my chocolate factory,' said Mr Wonka. 'Do you love it too, Charlie?'

'Oh, yes,' cried Charlie, 'it's the most wonderful place in the whole world.'

'Good,' said Mr Wonka, 'because it's YOURS!'

Charlie could not believe it. The chocolate factory was his!

The lift went down ...

down ...

CRASH

into Charlie's house!

'HELP!' cried Grandma Josephine.

'It's only us,' said Grandpa Joe.

'We're going to live in Charlie's chocolate factory. We'll never be hungry again!'

Before You Read

❶ Look at the cover. What do you think ? Answer Yes (Y), No (N), or Don't know (DK).

    a Are there any children in this story?

    b Are there any old people in this story?

    c Is this story about animals?

    d Is this story about a boy and a chocolate factory?

    e Will it be a sad story?

❷ Look through the book. Find the first names of these people in the story.

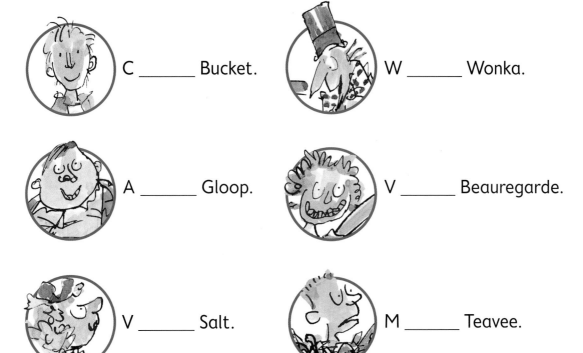

C _____ Bucket.

W _____ Wonka.

A _____ Gloop.

V _____ Beauregarde.

V _____ Salt.

M _____ Teavee.

After You Read

❶ Draw Charlie's family tree. Correct the names.

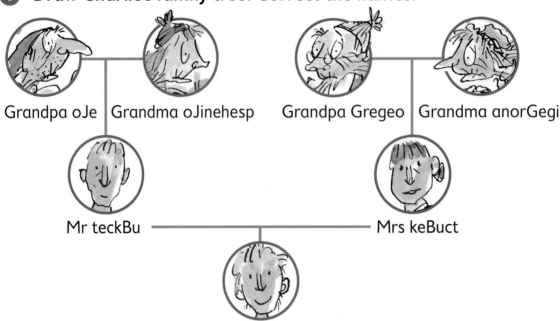

Grandpa oJe   Grandma oJinehesp   Grandpa Gregeo   Grandma anorGegi

Mr teckBu ———————————— Mrs keBuct

halCrie

❷ Write True (T) or False (F).

a Mr Wonka's factory made cars. ☐

b Six children found Golden Tickets. ☐

c Augustus was fat because he ate too much chocolate. ☐

d Violet liked chocolate better than gum. ☐

e Charlie fell down a hole in the Nut Room. ☐

f Mike got smaller and smaller in the Television Room. ☐

g The lift was made of chocolate. ☐